The Terrible
NUNG GWAMA

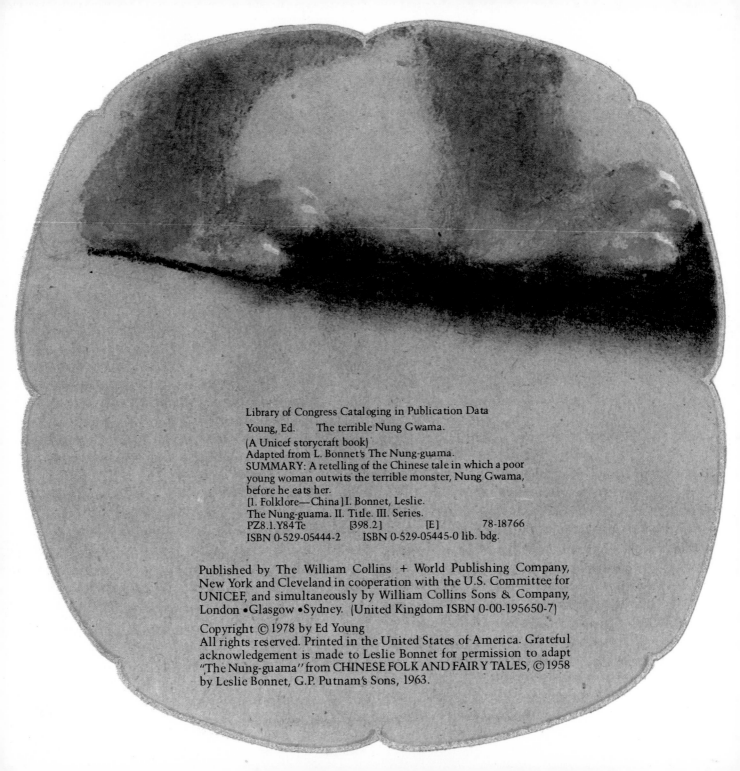

Library of Congress Cataloging in Publication Data

Young, Ed.   The terrible Nung Gwama.

(A Unicef storycraft book)
Adapted from L. Bonnet's The Nung-guama.
SUMMARY: A retelling of the Chinese tale in which a poor
young woman outwits the terrible monster, Nung Gwama,
before he eats her.
[1. Folklore—China] I. Bonnet, Leslie.
The Nung-guama. II. Title. III. Series.
PZ8.1.Y84Te   [398.2]   [E]   78-18766
ISBN 0-529-05444-2   ISBN 0-529-05445-0 lib. bdg.

Published by The William Collins + World Publishing Company,
New York and Cleveland in cooperation with the U.S. Committee for
UNICEF, and simultaneously by William Collins Sons & Company,
London •Glasgow •Sydney. (United Kingdom ISBN 0-00-195650-7)

A Chinese Folktale

The Terrible
NUNG GWAMA

ADAPTED BY ED YOUNG from the retelling by Leslie Bonnet

ILLUSTRATED BY ED YOUNG

COLLINS
+
WORLD
in cooperation with the U.S. Committee for UNICEF

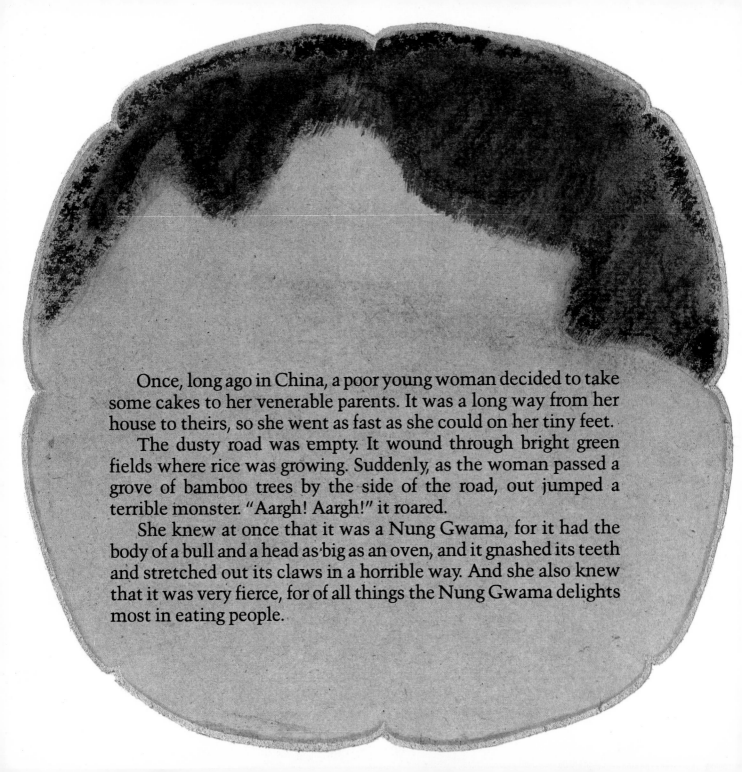

Once, long ago in China, a poor young woman decided to take some cakes to her venerable parents. It was a long way from her house to theirs, so she went as fast as she could on her tiny feet.

The dusty road was empty. It wound through bright green fields where rice was growing. Suddenly, as the woman passed a grove of bamboo trees by the side of the road, out jumped a terrible monster. "Aargh! Aargh!" it roared.

She knew at once that it was a Nung Gwama, for it had the body of a bull and a head as big as an oven, and it gnashed its teeth and stretched out its claws in a horrible way. And she also knew that it was very fierce, for of all things the Nung Gwama delights most in eating people.

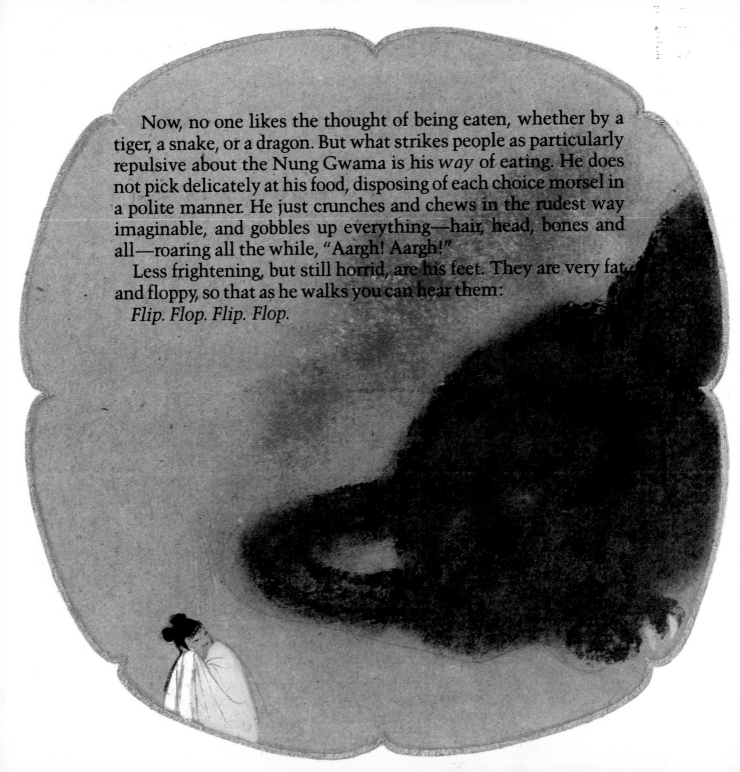

Now, no one likes the thought of being eaten, whether by a tiger, a snake, or a dragon. But what strikes people as particularly repulsive about the Nung Gwama is his *way* of eating. He does not pick delicately at his food, disposing of each choice morsel in a polite manner. He just crunches and chews in the rudest way imaginable, and gobbles up everything—hair, head, bones and all—roaring all the while, "Aargh! Aargh!"

Less frightening, but still horrid, are his feet. They are very fat and floppy, so that as he walks you can hear them:

Flip. Flop. Flip. Flop.

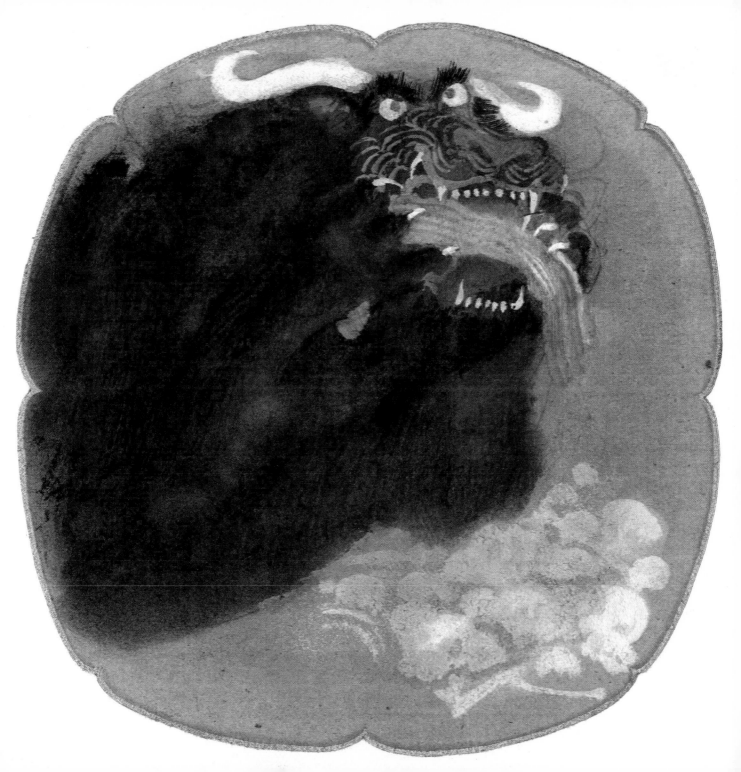

It was no wonder, then, that the poor woman sank to her knees in terror, and hid her face from this terrible monster.

The Nung Gwama said greedily, "Give me those delectable cakes at once."

Now, even though she was very frightened, the poor woman's duty to her parents came first.

"I can't do that," she said, sobbing. "They are for my venerable parents."

"All right, then," growled the Nung Gwama. "This very night I will come to your house and tear you to pieces with my claws and crunch you up with my sharp teeth and *eat* you."

At this, the woman hung her head in despair.

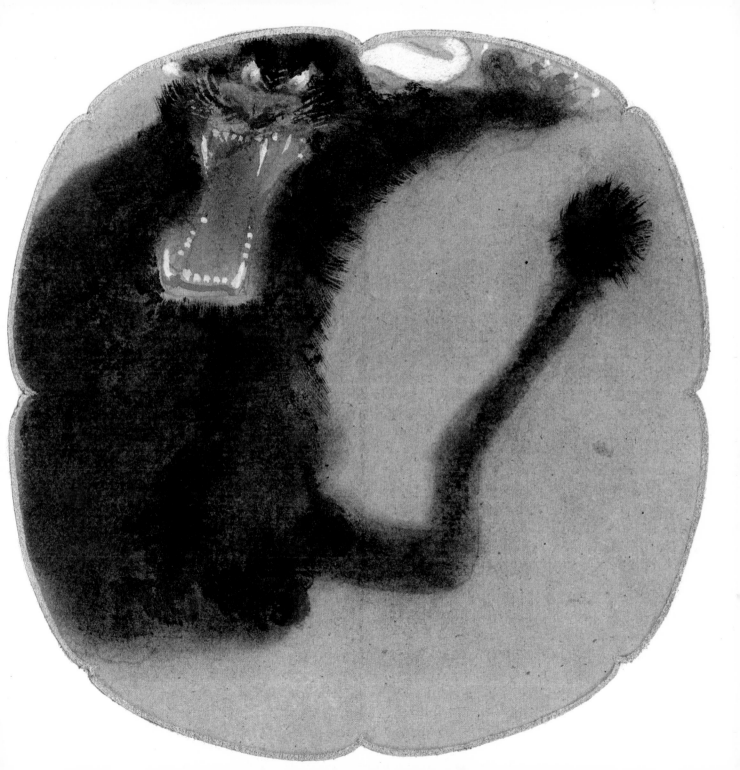

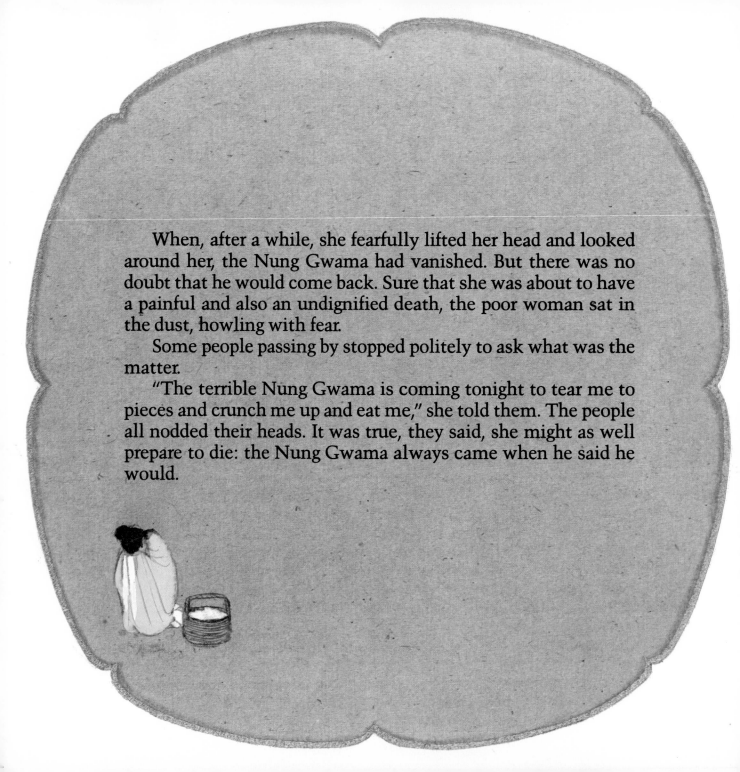

When, after a while, she fearfully lifted her head and looked around her, the Nung Gwama had vanished. But there was no doubt that he would come back. Sure that she was about to have a painful and also an undignified death, the poor woman sat in the dust, howling with fear.

Some people passing by stopped politely to ask what was the matter.

"The terrible Nung Gwama is coming tonight to tear me to pieces and crunch me up and eat me," she told them. The people all nodded their heads. It was true, they said, she might as well prepare to die: the Nung Gwama always came when he said he would.

While they were talking, a pedlar stopped to ask why the poor woman was weeping. They told him about the Nung Gwama's threat.

The pedlar set down the bamboo baskets which hung from his carrying pole. "Here," he said to the woman. "I'll give you twenty-four sharp needles. Stick them in the door of your house, near the latch. Maybe the Nung Gwama will prick himself when he tries to open the door." And the pedlar picked up his baskets and pole and went off again.

The woman, still frightened, continued to cry. For how could
a few needles save her from the Nung Gwama?

Her wails attracted a man who collected manure, which he used to fertilize his fields. He asked her what was the matter. When she told him, he thought for a while and then said, "Look, here is a little manure. Spread it on your door. Perhaps the Nung Gwama will dirty his hands with it, and go away."

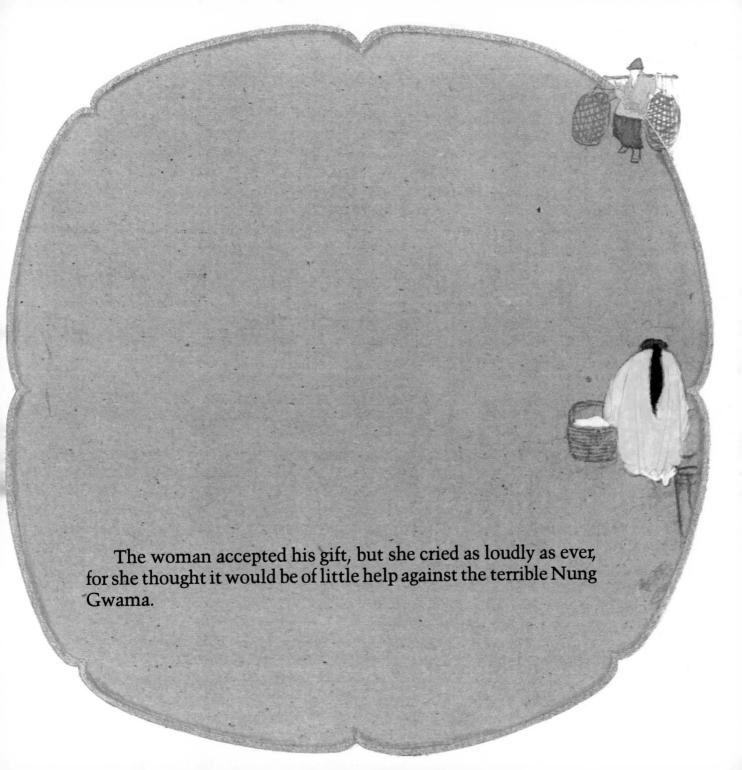

The woman accepted his gift, but she cried as loudly as ever, for she thought it would be of little help against the terrible Nung Gwama.

Soon a man came by, calling out, "Snakes for sale! Snakes for sale!" He, too, stopped when he saw the weeping woman. When he asked, she told him all about the Nung Gwama, the pedlar, and the man who collected manure.

The snake seller wanted to help her, too. "Here are two of my most poisonous snakes," he said. "Put them into your washing pot. Maybe the Nung Gwama will want to wash the manure off his hands. If he tries, these snakes will bite him."

The woman thanked him for his kindness, but she was soon weeping again—for what could mere snakes do against the terrible Nung Gwama?

Then a fish seller came along. "What is all this weeping and wailing?" he asked. The woman, still howling with fright, told him the whole story.

He, too, wanted to help. So he offered the woman two fish in a cooking pot. "Take these two fish," he said. "But don't cook them, or they won't be able to bite. Just keep them in the pot. If the Nung Gwama is bitten by the snakes, maybe he will think that the cooking pot is full of warm water and he will try to bathe his sore hands in it. If he puts his hands in the pot, the fish will bite him so hard he might give up the whole idea of eating you and run away."

The woman thought that was very unlikely, but she took the fish and the cooking pot and thanked him, and went on sobbing loudly.

An egg seller came by next, shouting, "Eggs! Fine eggs for sale!" He, too, asked what was wrong. When he was told, he scratched his head and thought very hard. Then he said, "You must take these few eggs. Put them in the ashes of your fire. If the Nung Gwama is bitten by the snakes and the fish, his fingers will bleed. Then he will want to put them in the ashes to stop the bleeding. If he does that, the eggs will burst in his face. That should scare him out of his wickedness."

The woman did not think it would be so easy to scare the terrible Nung.Gwama, but she thanked him and took the eggs, and then she cried louder than ever.

Next, a seller of millstones heard her crying. "I will give you this millstone," he said to her. "It is very, very heavy. You must hang it from the ceiling above your bed. If you can get the Nung Gwama to stand below it, cut the string and maybe the millstone will fall on the monster's head and knock him out. But then it may still be necessary to finish him off, so here is an iron bar with which you can beat out any life that is left in him."

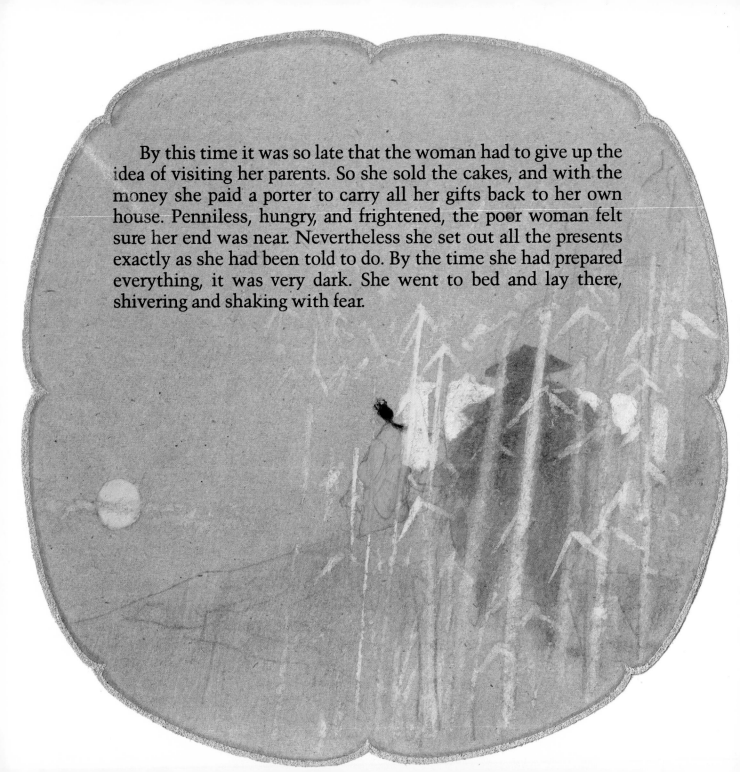

By this time it was so late that the woman had to give up the idea of visiting her parents. So she sold the cakes, and with the money she paid a porter to carry all her gifts back to her own house. Penniless, hungry, and frightened, the poor woman felt sure her end was near. Nevertheless she set out all the presents exactly as she had been told to do. By the time she had prepared everything, it was very dark. She went to bed and lay there, shivering and shaking with fear.

But nothing happened. The old watchman went by, calling out the first and second watches of the night. Then he passed by again, tapping his drum for the third watch and calling out a warning to robbers.

Still nothing happened. Everything was quiet.

Then suddenly—*Flip. Flop. Flip. Flop.* It was the fat and floppy feet of the Nung Gwama, and they were just outside the door!

"*Aargh! Aargh!* Open up the door," roared the Nung Gwama. "I have come to tear you and crunch you and eat you all up."

The woman could not move, she was so frightened. The Nung Gwama rushed at the door and tore it down. But as he did, the twenty-four needles stuck in his hands and the manure dirtied them.

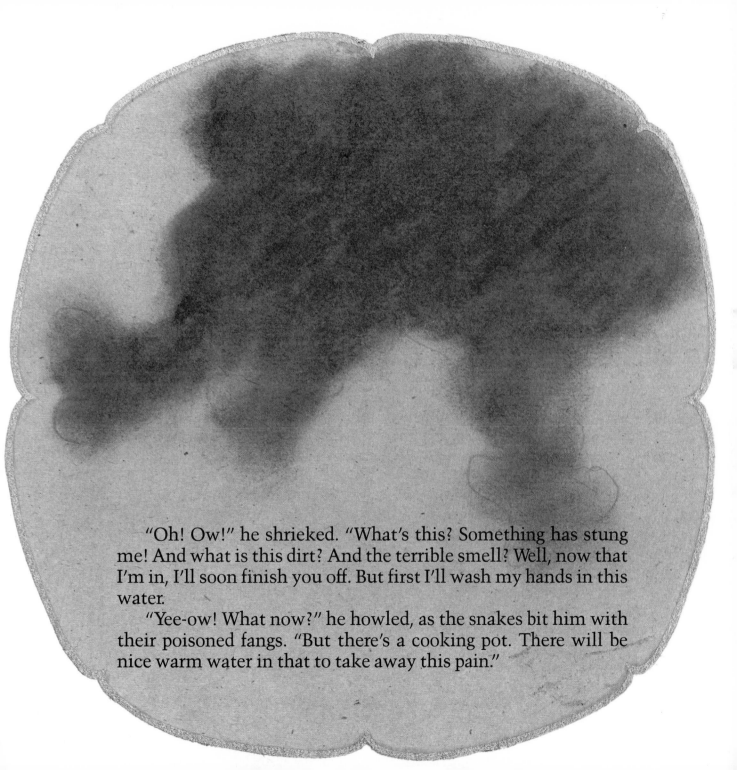

"Oh! Ow!" he shrieked. "What's this? Something has stung me! And what is this dirt? And the terrible smell? Well, now that I'm in, I'll soon finish you off. But first I'll wash my hands in this water.

"Yee-ow! What now?" he howled, as the snakes bit him with their poisoned fangs. "But there's a cooking pot. There will be nice warm water in that to take away this pain."

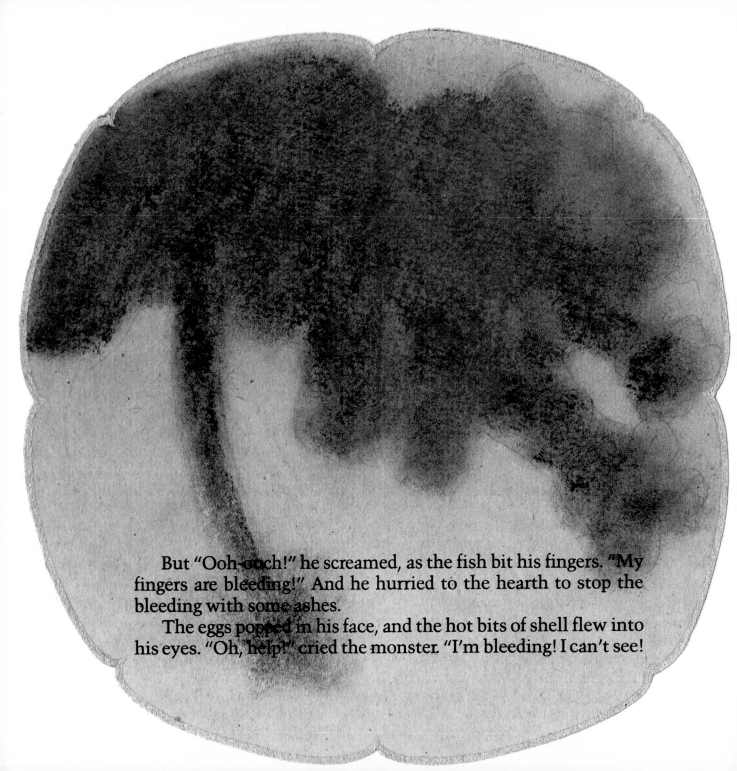

But "Ooh-ouch!" he screamed, as the fish bit his fingers. "My fingers are bleeding!" And he hurried to the hearth to stop the bleeding with some ashes.

The eggs popped in his face, and the hot bits of shell flew into his eyes. "Oh, help!" cried the monster. "I'm bleeding! I can't see!

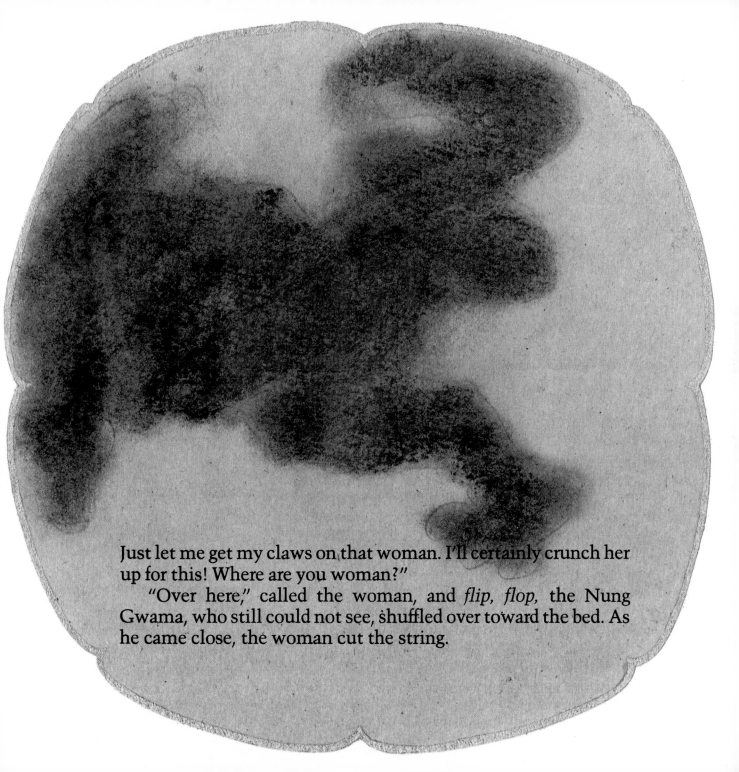

Just let me get my claws on that woman. I'll certainly crunch her up for this! Where are you woman?"

"Over here," called the woman, and *flip, flop*, the Nung Gwama, who still could not see, shuffled over toward the bed. As he came close, the woman cut the string.

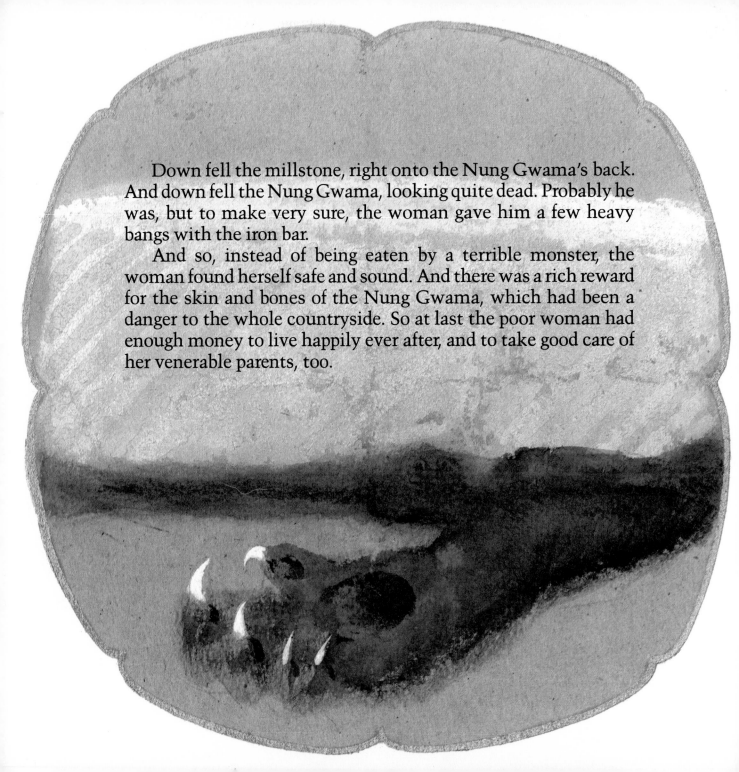

Down fell the millstone, right onto the Nung Gwama's back. And down fell the Nung Gwama, looking quite dead. Probably he was, but to make very sure, the woman gave him a few heavy bangs with the iron bar.

And so, instead of being eaten by a terrible monster, the woman found herself safe and sound. And there was a rich reward for the skin and bones of the Nung Gwama, which had been a danger to the whole countryside. So at last the poor woman had enough money to live happily ever after, and to take good care of her venerable parents, too.

About Ed Young

Ed Young is particularly known for his unique talent for creating modern versions of ancient or traditional art forms of the Near and Far East. Included among the many beautiful books he has illustrated are THE EMPEROR AND THE KITE, a Caldecott Honor Book (written by Jane Yolen) the pictures for which are created in colored papercuts; THE GIRL WHO LOVED THE WIND, also by Jane Yolen, in a style inspired by Persian miniatures of the Moghul period; THE ROOSTER'S HORNS, a shadow puppet play which tells in words and pictures how children can enjoy and perform this traditional Chinese craft in their own homes; and now THE TERRIBLE NUNG GWAMA, which grew out of his desire to bring the robust spirit and wit, as well as the beauty of Chinese folktales to young readers. Born in Shanghai, China, he now lives in the United States. A graduate of the Los Angeles Art Center, he has taught art at Yale University and at Pratt Institute of Art; he also has taught Tai Chi Chuan at the New York Tai Chi Chuan Cooperative.

About this story

A popular Chinese folktale, THE TERRIBLE NUNG GWAMA comes from Kuang-tung province in Southern China. It is one of many tales and songs brought to light by Hu Shih when he and other Chinese nationalists sought to establish the *pai-hua*, or colloquial language, as the base of a national literature of the common people, in order to free the emerging China from the bonds of a restrictive, classical past. Acceptance of their own rich and eloquent peasant folklore became a national cause as China made its transition from the traditions of the past into the modern world. Now scholars and folklorists are beginning to bring to other nations these beautiful songs and tales reflective of Chinese culture.

This particular version of the story of the Nung Gwama is adapted by Ed Young from a retelling by the well-known British storyteller Leslie Bonnet, who discovered it in an earlier, scholarly translation of the tales collected by Hu Shih and his collaborators. Though retold, both versions remain faithful to the original.